Keeping secrets

I was asleep having a great erotic dream until I woke up prematurely. I jumped out of bed and got into the shower to get rid of my never-ending boner. The only problem was that today it was not working.

My roommate Amy came into my bathroom. I said hey Amy what's up. She said oh wow nice big black cock. I said thanks Amy what's up. She said your girlfriend is calling on your cell phone.

I said I'll have to call her back later. I need to get rid of this never-ending boner. Amy said I can give you a hand job. I said but you have a boyfriend. Amy said I love keeping dirty secrets.

I said in that case stroke away Amy. She grabbed my black cock and started stroking. Her white hands looked and felt great on my hard-black cock. I noticed Amy wearing a sexy short night gown.

It really turned me on as she stroked my hard cock. Amy smiled and said I love your big cock, it's really beautiful. I said thanks you have wonderful hands.

Amy said thanks I aim to please you. I finally felt that amazing feeling. Amy was not paying attention. I sprayed her sexy nightgown with my orgasmic cream.

I said oh crap sorry Amy, she said its ok I love being sprayed by a man's hard cock. I said thanks for the help Amy. She said my pleasure stroking your big hard wonderful black cock.

I smiled and Amy walked out as I watched her sexy big ass jiggled out of the room. I finished my shower and hopped out of the shower. I called my girlfriend Amber.

I said sorry I was in the shower when you called that's when she said can I come over. I'm horny I said sure baby come on over. She said I'll see you after work. I said cool and I went to work too.

After work I went home and waited for Amber to come over. I opened the door, she hugged and kissed me immediately. We went to my bedroom, Amber stripped out of all her clothes and jumped on the bed.

She said pound me big daddy. I said with pleasure, I got naked and jumped on her sexy ass. I kissed her passionately and plunged my love dagger into her pleasure palace.

Amber said oh baby you always give me what I need. I held her tight and rammed the shit out of her horny pussy. Amber gave up the cream willingly and frequently.

I said bend that big ass over and let me work on that pussy baby. Amber bent over, I pulled her hair and took her roughly from behind. Amber loves that shit a lot, she creamed my dick twice as I pounded her pussy.

I kept up the pace until I ejaculated into Amber's tight little cunt. I smacked her ass and said that's my horny little slut. Amber said I'll always be your little slut my stud.

We made out then fell asleep. We woke up and it was nighttime. We went to the couch to watch television. Amber was wearing my shirt and cuddled up to me.

Amy came out and said hey guys what's up. Amber said hey Amy and they hugged, two hot white bitches hugging that is so hot. Amy sat beside me and we watched television together like normal.

I was sandwiched by sweet white thighs on both sides. I made it through the movie, later Amber and I went to my bedroom to sleep. The next morning Amber and I were in the kitchen. I said how about a blow job baby. Amber said ok then got on her knees then put my dick in her mouth.

She started blowing my cock like crazy, I held on to the counter for dear life. I moaned and let my sperm explode into Amber's warm mouth. I said oh yeah baby I love when you suck me dry. Amber swallowed and was licking my cockhead clean when Amy walked in and said oh my god, I'm so sorry. Amber said its ok I was just sucking him dry. Amy said that's a big fucking dick. Amber said I know I can't seem to keep it out of my mouth or pussy.

I said I love my horny girlfriend. Amber said I love you too baby. Amy said I don't blame you if my boyfriend had a big cock like that, I'd be all over it too. I smiled at Amy when she said that to Amber.

We sat down to eat breakfast, Amy said are we going to church today. Amber said I don't have anything to wear. Amy said we are the same size; I think you can find something in my closet that you can wear. We finished our breakfast then they went to Amy's closet.

Twenty minutes later, both came out wearing sexy short dresses. I said wow you look incredible Amber, she said thank you baby. I said you look great too Amy. She said thanks roomy. I said let's get to church before we are late.

We walked into church holding hands. The ladies were looking at Amy and Amber in their sexy outfits. I know they are jealous of my two horny white girls. We sat down to enjoy the mass, remembering this is a judgy society hear in Salt Lake City, Utah.

We were sitting normally with me admiring both of their sweet white thighs when Amber whispered in my ears that she and Amy were not wearing panties or bras. I said praise the lord. Amy and Amber said amen. I smiled and they giggled, the judgy crew in church gave us the stink eye treatment.

After the church sermon we mingled with our fellow parishioners, the guys were checking out Amy and Amber's sexy outfits while their wives and girlfriends were hitting them for looking at the two curvaceous pleasures on my arm.

Afterwards, we left to go back home. During the car ride home, I said I think the ladies at the church really liked your outfits. Amber and Amy laughed out loud. Amy said they are just jealous they can't dress sexy; they are too uptight. I said do you guys know any good proctologists. Both Amy and Amber laughed out loud as I smiled at my funny joke.

Amber said they would all have a heart attack if they knew we were not wearing panties or bras. Amy said only the women the men might like it laughing. I said I liked knowing it, Amber said did it make your big cock hard during church. I said oh yeah. Amy said so that's why you didn't go to communion.

I said exactly, I think people might have noticed a big tent in my pants. Amy and Amber both laughed out loud. We arrived home and hung out the rest of the day watching football.

After football, Amber left thanking Amy for lending her the dress. She said I'll wash it and bring it back. Amy said thanks I'll see you later. She left I said that was hot knowing that you were not wearing underwear in church. Amy said I was wet the whole time never did anything like that before so naughty. I said I agree very naughty Amy, bad girl. She smiled ear to ear at me.

The next day I came home from work and I was on the couch jerking off when Amy came home. Amy said do you need a hand baby. I said sure if you don't mind. Amy put her things down and started stroking my hard cock. It felt great with her warm hands on my hard cock.

Amy said you know I'll be happy to give you a hand job anytime you want right. I said really you don't mind. Amy said not at all I love keeping dirty secrets from your girlfriend Amber and my boyfriend Anthony.

Amy looked me in the eyes as she stroked my cock up and down. I said thanks for doing this, Amy said my pleasure stroking you're really nice dick. I felt too good moaning louder and louder as Amy sped up the pace.

She had her mouth wide open stroking my cock like crazy. I said how about a blow job Amy. She said sure another dirty secret. Amy put my cock in her wonderful mouth and started sucking like crazy. I said oh yeah white girl suck that black dick and she sucked it harder.

Moments later, I spilled my seed in her warm mouth. Amy swallowed all of it and my eyes almost popped out of my head. I said wow you swallowed all of it. Amy said yeah does that turn you on, I said hell yeah.

Amy said I'm still horny do you mind fingering me. I said sure, she took my finger and sucked it like she was sucking my dick. Amy stood up and put my hand between her sweet white thighs. She moved her panties to the side and I pushed my finger in her wet pussy.

Amy squeezed her big titties as I fingered her white pussy. I sped up my pace and Amy moaned louder. Moments later she screamed with pleasure as she came all over my finger. I said oh yeah baby cream that fucking finger.

I held my finger in her pussy until she came down from her euphoric high. Amy said thanks I really appreciate that, sucking your dick made me very horny. I said my pleasure anytime you need to be fingered let me know. Amy said oh yeah, I will definitely let you know, your long ass fingers are magical in my white pussy.

The following evening, I climbed into my bed naked ready to sleep when Amy came to my room totally naked. I said hi Amy nice body. She giggled and said thanks stud. I said what's up sexy. Amy said I'm ready to keep the most forbidden of secrets your big black cock deep in my white pussy.

I said get into my bed and I will take good care of you Amy. She climbed into my bed and kissed me. I rolled on top of her kissing her passionately. I grind my hard-black cock on her wet white pussy.

I could feel her wetness lubricating my cock shaft. Amy whispered in my ears fuck me and make me your little white slut. I held my cock pushed it in her white pussy with a lot of force because it would not go in her tight white pussy gently.

I squeezed Amy's big tits and fucked her hard. Amy moaned and said I've always wanted to get fucked by a black man. I said it's my pleasure to break you in baby. I kissed Amy again and she held me tight. Amy said fuck me until you spill your warm seed in my white vagina.

I fucked Amy harder and harder until I got that wonderful feeling. I said hear it comes baby and Amy said yes. I felt her cream on my cock just before I released my seed into her warm horny vagina.

Amy said don't get off I want to stay this way until you go soft. I want to savor my first time with a black stud. I smiled and kissed her. We held each other for a long time.

Amy finally let me go and said I better get to my bed. I said stay here my little white slut. Amy giggled and said sure my stud. We cuddled up and slept naked together.

My cellphone rang and it was my girlfriend Amber calling to talk to me. Amy woke up too. I said its Amber, I said hey sweetie what's up. Amy snuggled up to me naked as I talked to my girlfriend Amber.

Amy stayed quiet smiling as I talked to my girlfriend. Amber said just calling to say I love you and I miss you. I said I love you and I miss you too baby. I said my cock misses you and Amber said my white pussy misses your black pole deep in it. I said I can't with to fuck you as Amy rubbed her pussy on my leg while rubbing my hard cock. When I got off the phone with my girlfriend.

Amy said how about a quickie before we go to work. I said ok bend over. Amy bent over and said I like being your little white slut. I plunged my cock into Amy's wet vagina. I held her hips and pounded the shit out of her horny pussy.

I tore her white pussy up, Amy screamed and her pussy vibrated. She creamed my dick just before I exploded in her horny cunt. I smack her sexy big ass and said don't be late for work sweet cheeks. Amy said yes sir.

We hugged and kiss then Amy jiggled her sexy ass to her bedroom as I watched. I showered and went to work. Amber's sister Amanda texted me asking if I wanted to do lunch. I said sure, we set up a lunch date and I went to see Amanda.

We hugged and sat down in a booth next to each other to eat lunch. Amanda was wearing a short ass skirt that showed off her sweet white thighs.

I said you look great Amanda in that short ass skirt. Amanda giggled and said I just wanted you to notice me. I said I noticed, I reached down and rubbed her sweet white thighs. She said oh my god your rubbing my white thighs don't tell my boyfriend I let you rub my white thighs. I said it will be our dirty little secret.

I went higher massaging her thighs and Amanda willingly spread her sweet white thighs for me. I felt her wet pussy, I said how come your white pussy is wet. Amanda said a sexy black man is rubbing my white thighs and my white pussy that's why I'm soaking wet and horny.

I said will you let your sister's black boyfriend fuck your sweet white pussy. Amanda shook her head then said I want you too. I whispered in her ear that we can eat first then go fuck in her apartment close by since her boyfriend Adrian is away on a business trip.

Our meals came and we thanked the waitress. We ate looking and smiling at each other the whole time. I was very excited to fuck Amanda for the first time. We have been flirting for a while now building up our courage, now the lust is flowing between both of us.

We finished our meals and I paid the bill leaving a huge tip to the hot waitress Abigail. We walked to her apartment separately. I waited five minutes then I went up to her apartment. Amanda opened the door. I went in and we closed the door. I kissed her up against the door, I reached between her sweet white thighs and stuck my finger in her pussy.

Amanda took my cock out and stroked it. I kissed her neck and lifted her up on the door. I slowly slid her white pussy down my big cock. Amanda said oh my god your black cock is so big and deep in my white pussy.

I started sliding my black wood in and out of Amanda's white pussy. Amanda moaned with pleasure as I gave it to her. She said I've wanted your black penetration for so long. I said I've wanted to penetrate your sweet white pussy ever since your sister introduced us.

I carried hot Amanda to the couch. I fucked her harder and sucked on her big titties. I kissed her and held her tight as I pounded her into the couch with vigor. Amanda moaned oh god I'm coming on your huge fucking cock. I said oh yeah Amanda come on your sisters boyfriends black cock.

She smiled at me and said spill your seed in your girlfriend's sisters pussy. I said with pleasure and I gave her ten more hard strokes then let my seed flow into Amanda's pussy. I moaned oh god I loved fucking your forbidden white pussy.

Amanda said I love your forbidden black cock and your sperm in my horny cunt. We kissed and cuddled for a while. I said I better get back to work. Amanda said me too. We put our clothes back on freshened up and went back to work.

A week later, I was on top of Amy slowly sliding my black cock in and out of her white pussy. Amy cell phone rang and she said don't stop fucking me. It's my mom she is cool. Amy answered her cell with a video call, hi mom what's up. I smiled as I massaged her white pussy with my black penis while she talked to her mom.

Amber moaned then her mom Ashley said are you ok. Amber said yeah, I'm ok then she moaned again. Ashley said what are you doing I want the truth. Amber said I'm getting fucked by my handsome roommate's huge black cock.

Ashley said oh my god my white daughter is getting fucked by a big black cock. She said can I see his black pole; I've never seen a big black cock before in my life. Amber said take it out my mom wants to see your huge black cock.

I took it out and rubbed Amy's clit with my cock head. Ashley said oh my god sir you have a beautiful black cock. I said thank you Ashley and she said thank you for showing me your black cock, now put it back in my white daughter and fuck her until you spill your seed in her.

I slid my black pole back in Amy and fucked her hard. Amy moaned when she creamed my cock and soon after she came, I spilled my seed in her horny pussy with her mom watching. I moaned oh Ashley I'm coming in your hot daughter as I deposited my pleasure cream in her white vagina.

I took my cock out and squeezed out the last drop and rubbed it on Amy's clit. Ashley said wow you came in my daughter. Amy said oh yeah, he did and Ashley said does your boyfriend know your fucking your roommate.

Amy said oh hell no and his girlfriend doesn't know that I'm giving it up to him. Ashley said wow dirty secrets I love it. I kissed and held Amy as she said goodbye to her mom. I said bye Ashley and she said bye stud.

I said that's pretty kinky your mom watching us fuck and have orgasms. Amy said oh yeah very kinky my mom is cool. She likes younger men but hasn't built up the courage to fuck one yet. I said oh wow.

A month later, Ashley texted me asking where her daughter Amy was and that she was in the neighborhood. I said she went out with her boyfriend. I thought that was the end of it, minutes later I heard our doorbell rang.

It was Ashley, Amy's mom in a sexy short dress. I became very aroused opening the door. I said come on in and I closed the door behind her. Ashley came in for a hug and I was hard already. I could feel my hard-black cock pressing against Ashley's pussy.

The hot mom of Amy looked amazing. We went to the couch to sit down. I said can I get you something. Ashley said water would be nice. I got her some water. She looked nervous drinking the water.

I said I love your dress Ashley as I admired her sweet white thighs. Ashley looked at my bulge in my pants and bit her blow job lips. I said you have some sweet ass white thighs. Ashley giggled and turned red.

I rubbed her sweet white thighs and Ashley moaned with pleasure. She spread her thighs and I saw her red see through panties covering her shaved white pussy. My cock pulsated at the sight of it. I leaned in and kissed Ashley. She put her arms around me and kissed me back.

We fell over into a great make out session. I was on top of Ashley grinding my cock into her pussy kissing her pretty neck. I said I want you Ashley and she said I want your black penetration.

I pulled down my pants and moved her panties to the side and slammed my black cock up her white pussy. Ashley moaned oh god yes finally some young cock in my white pussy. I held her tight as I pounded Ashley's white pussy.

She gave up the pleasure cream willingly and frequently as I pounded her into the couch. I said your so sexy Ashley. She said you are a very handsome black man with a huge fucking cock.

I moaned then let my seed spill into Amy's hot mom's married pussy. I kissed Ashley and we held each other tightly. I said did you enjoy it baby. Ashely said oh yeah, I've never felt more alive getting boned by a hot young stud.

I smiled at her and my cell rang. It was her daughter Amy calling to tell me that she was not coming home tonight. I said cool I will see you when I see you then.

I said do you want to spend the night Ashley; Amy is with her boyfriend and my girlfriend Amber is visiting her mother. Ashley said sure I'd love to spend the night with my new young black lover.

Ashley made us dinner in her panties and bra as I watched her sexy body work. We sat and ate smiling, then she said I have been obsessed with younger men for years but this is the first time that I've acted upon it and I'm glad I did it with such a handsome black stud muffin.

I said I'm glad that you acted upon it, you are one hot ass sexy milf. Ashley smiled and turned red with embarrassment. We ate the wonderful dinner that she created for us of steak, fries and mash potatoes.

After dinner, we relaxed on the couch talking dirty to each other. Ashley and I were looking at each other and smiling when she leaned in and kissed me. She climbed on my lap straddling me, I took off her bra and sucked her big titties.

Ashley said I love my big titties sucked on and squeezed. I was sucking the hell out of her big tits when she took my hard cock out and slid down it, moaning with pleasure.

She rode my black cock slowly as I sucked on her melons. Her daughter Amy called her cell phone, Ashley stopped as my hard cock pulsated in her white pussy. I gently sucked her melons as she talked to her daughter. I noticed she didn't mention my black cock in her white pussy.

It was a brief check in with her daughter, she hung up and said where were we. I said how come you don't want your daughter to know you are getting young black cock deep in your horny white pussy.

Ashley said I've always wanted to have a secret black lover. I said I'm honored to be your secret black lover. I was still turned on and Ashley started to ride me again this time with more ferocity.

Ashley worked my dick over pretty good and a few minutes later. I saw her eyes roll back in her head and I felt extra lubrication on my cock. She screamed out in pleasure. Moments later I said here it comes baby as I release my pleasure cream inside of Ashley's forbidden married pussy.

We kissed as secret lovers on the couch then I took Ashley to my shower. I soaped up Ashley's big titties and juicy ass while she soaped up my hard cock. We were rinsing off when Ashley got on her knees and put my black cock in her hot mouth.

I held her head as she took me on a great blow job ride of pleasure with a lot of teasing and sucking until I couldn't take it anymore and released into her wonderful mouth. Ashley sucked all of my sperm down her throat to my delightful ecstasy.

Unfortunately, Ashley had to go, we hugged and kissed passionately at the door before we said our goodbyes. Amy came home and I was in bed watching television. She stripped naked and joined me in bed. We were kissing when she said whose red panties are these.

I said it was Amber's red panties, when I knew full well it was her mother's Ashley red panties. I took them from her and put them under my pillow for safe keeping. Amber cuddled up naked with me, I said how was your weekend with your boyfriend.

Amy said great, we had a lot of sex. My mom called me when I was coming back to our apartment. She said who would you marry, the handsome black roommate with the huge cock or your white boyfriend. I laughed and said your mom is pretty hot I wonder if she likes black cock.

Amy giggled and said I'd love to see you fuck my married mom with your huge black cock. I said oh wow really, I'd love it more. Amy said that would be the most forbidden of secrets to keep from my dad. I said yes indeed, too bad I can't tell Amy that I fucked her hot mom Ashley and she is an excellent roll in the hay.

The end

www.ingramcontent.com/pod-product-compliance
Ingram Content Group UK Ltd.
Pitfield, Milton Keynes, MK11 3LW, UK
UKHW022008190726
13853UKWH00004B/1804

9 798773 842651